CONDENSED BOOK

For Bili
with
condensed
regards

Peti Cherp

CONDENSED BOOK
Peter Cherches

BENZENE EDITIONS
NEW YORK 1986

Some of the pieces in this volume
have appeared in the following
publications: *Benzene, Junction,
New Leaves Review, Five Plus Five.*

Bagatelles was originally
published in 1981 by Benzene
Editions.

Unfamiliar Tales was originally
published in 1982 by Purgatory
Pie Press.

ISBN 0-939194-03-1

Benzene Editions
P.O. Box 383
New York, N.Y. 10014

CONTENTS

BAGATELLES

Lift your right arm, she said.
I lifted my right arm.
Lift your left arm, she said.
I lifted my left arm. Both of my arms were up.
Put down your right arm, she said.
I put it down.
Put down your left arm, she said.
I did.
Lift your right arm, she said.
I obeyed.
Put down your right arm.
I did.
Lift your left arm.
I lifted it.
Put down your left arm.
I did.

Silence. I stood there, both arms down, waiting for her next command. After a while I got impatient and said, what next.

Now it's your turn to give the orders, she said.

All right, I said. Tell me to lift my right arm.

Her voice. It ruled me. Not she, not by any measure. But her voice, when it chose to speak to me.

She was a constant. I used her to gauge reality. The world existed for me in relation to her. For instance, I used her as a standard for temperature. For the sake of convenience, I called her body temperature zero. For us to be comfortable, room temperature had to be considerably below zero. And when she had a fever it had to be even colder.

I often told myself, were it not for her I would be alone. I often told myself, were it not for me she would be alone. I often told myself, one should not be alone. I often told her, one should not be alone. I often asked myself, could I live without her. I often asked her, could you live without me. She often said yes, she often said no.

Yes, I told her, yes, if that's what you'd like. Yes, she said, I would like it, I would like it very much. Very well then, I said, if that's what you'd like, if that's what you'd like then most certainly. Most certainly that's what I'd like, she said, most certainly I'd like that very much. Very well, I said, most certainly, yes. Oh thank you, she said, thank you very much.

Sniffing each other was our favorite pastime. We would produce various and sundry odors for each other's benefit. Some of our odors were mutual, but certainly not all. She produced many odors which I could not duplicate, and vice-versa. We spent many pleasant hours producing odors for each other. When we became familiar with each other's repertoire of odors, we began to make requests. It was pure ecstasy. When we were sniffing each other nothing else mattered. We had each other, and as far as we were concerned, who cared how the world smelled.

You take a lot out of me, she said to me.
I know, I told her in her own voice.

I hear a noise, she said. I don't, I said. I definitely hear a noise, she said. I don't, I said. You must be deaf, she said. Describe the noise, I said. I can't, she said. What does it sound like, I said. I understood you the first time, she said. And, I said. And I can't describe what it sounds like, she said. Show me then, I said. She did. I don't hear a thing, I said. You must be deaf, she said. Try again, I said. She did. Well, she said. I still don't hear a thing, I said. You only hear what you want to hear, she said.

Where is she, I wondered, when she wasn't there. If she's not here she could be anywhere. She could be anywhere and not alone.

I began to imagine the worst. At every imagining I thought I had imagined the worst, then I imagined something even worse. It got to the point where my imaginings no longer included her. I realized that the worst did not encompass her. As my imaginings continued, as worst superseded worst, making the preceding worst only worse, I began to forget her. As worst got worse, I forgot her more. Things were getting pretty bad, and I had almost forgotten her completely, when she reappeared.

Our life together has its limits, I said.

What exactly do you mean, she said.

Our life together is limited in time and space, I said.

Oh, she said.

I said something which she obviously misinterpreted, because she reacted angrily. She was screaming, in a frenzy. I couldn't get a word in edgewise. I let her go on until she ran out of steam. When I was sure she was through, I repeated my original statement. She must have understood this time because she said, oh yes, now I understand.

I had a dream. About her. I dreamed that she wasn't there. Only I was there. I was there, knowing that she wasn't there. I was dreaming knowing that she wasn't there. She wasn't there, and I knew it. I dreamed knowing it. I woke up thinking it. But she was there. I saw that she was there. We were both there. I was there, awake, knowing that she was there. And she was there, asleep, dreaming.

Once, while I was licking her, she disappeared. I knew she had disappeared because my tongue was lapping at the air. I was distressed, but I kept on licking. I licked for some time, until I felt her body once again on my tongue.

Let me do your portrait, I said. All right, she said.

She sat for me.

I didn't have a pen. All I had was a blank sheet of paper.

I looked at her, and then at the paper. I looked at the paper for a while, then back at her. Then back at the paper. Back at her. At the paper. Her. The paper. I looked at the paper for some time, then I showed it to her.

It doesn't look anything like me, she said.

It's an idealization, I said.

You're ugly, I told her. Yesterday you said I was beautiful, she said. Yesterday you were beautiful, I said. And today, she said. Today you're ugly, I said.

The next day I told her she was beautiful. Yesterday you said I was ugly, she said. Yesterday you were ugly, I said. And today, she said. Today you're beautiful, I said.

The day after that I told her she was ugly. Yesterday you said I was beautiful, and the day before you said I was ugly, and the day before that you said I was beautiful, she said. Yesterday you were beautiful, two days ago you were ugly, and three days ago you were beautiful, I said. And today, she said. Today you're ugly, I said.

The following day I told her she was ugly. You told me I was ugly yesterday too, she said. Pardon me, I said, I forgot what day it was.

There's something missing from our relation-
ship, she said.
Do you know what it is, I said.
It could be anything, she said.

We had been together for some time by this time. Many years. We had stopped counting. We celebrated anniversaries, but as far as we were concerned each anniversary meant just another year. We kept records, of course, and had we wanted to know we could certainly have looked it up, but neither of us ever did. Sometimes, however, the subject did come up. This was inevitable. For instance, we would have a fight and she would say, it's been many years, hasn't it. And I, still in the spirit of combat, would say, yes, many, indeed. Or, feeling a bit nostalgic she would say, it's been many years, hasn't it. And I, caught up in the spirit of nostalgia, would say, yes, many, indeed. And, occasionally, simply musing about time and the two of us, she would say, it's been many years, hasn't it. And I, similarly musing about the two of us and time, would say, yes, many, indeed. It's been many years.

You're a prick, she said. You're a cunt, I said. You're a prick, she said. You're a cunt, I said. You're a prick, she said. You're a cunt, I said. I forgot what we're arguing about, she said. Pricks and cunts, I said.

We decided to try something new.

Afterwards, I asked her what she thought.

It seemed familiar, she said. Are you sure we've never done that before.

Positive.

It seemed so familiar. I think we did something like it a long time ago.

I know what you're thinking of, I said. But it wasn't exactly the same thing.

I had nothing to be afraid of: There was only one of her, but there were two of us.

We were going over snapshots, having decided to look back at the past. As we never had a camera, we had only the snapshots of memory. We passed them between us.

Remember this one, she would say, and tell me what she was thinking of. Ah, yes, I would reply with a smile. How about this one, I would say, and tell her mine. Do I ever, she would say, and laugh. We went over hundreds of these pictures, and what memories they brought back. At one point, though, she brought up one that I couldn't seem to place. I don't remember that one, I told her. She thought about it for a few moments and then said, no, come to think of it, neither do I.

She was lying motionless. I went over and kicked her, not too hard, just hard enough to see if she was still alive. She was, because she moved in a certain way. That's good, I thought, because if she's still alive it means that we can resume.

I sat for a while and she walked. Then she got tired and sat, so I walked. I walked for a while, then I told her I wanted to sit, so she got up and walked again. I sat there, watching her walk, remembering how we used to walk together.

We tried to put each other into words. But words weren't enough. So we put each other into sentences. No good. Paragraphs. Unsatisfactory. Chapters. Not quite right. A book. Books. Volume upon volume upon volume. It just wouldn't work. Nothing was enough, everything was too much.

I created you out of nothingness, and I can annihilate you any time I feel like it, I told her.

I'd like to see you try, she said.

A SHORT NAP

I was hired to keep an eye on them. I was hired to watch them, to listen to them. They hired me. He hired me to watch her. She hired me to watch him. They hired me to watch each other.

I'm no detective. I'm no dick, no shamus. Just a guy who needed a job.

I didn't ask any questions. He approached me first and I didn't ask any questions. I didn't ask any questions when she approached me, after him. You just don't ask questions.

He approached me first. He explained the whole thing, and there was nothing to explain. Just keep an eye on her, and don't ask any questions. Don't make any judgments, don't come to any conclusions, just keep an eye on her.

She said the same thing, only in different words. Just keep an eye on him and don't ask any questions. Just keep an eye on him and don't make any judgments, don't bother with conclusions.

Will do, I said. Will do, I told him. Will do, I told her. And don't worry, I told them both, so they wouldn't worry.

He approached first, she approached next. Keep an eye on her, keep an eye on him. Will do, will do.

It was a job. That's all it was to me. A job. Money. Cash up front. More to come. If I did a good job. A good job. Whatever that meant.

We discussed money. I discussed money with him first. There wasn't much to say. I told him what I wanted. He told me what he had. I told him what I needed. He told me what he'd give me. I told him I'd take it.

I discussed money with her next. We talked figures. I told her I liked hers. She told me I was fresh. I told her what I wanted. She told me I couldn't have it. I told her what I needed. She told me what she'd give me. I told her I'd take it.

I took it. I took it from him, I took it from her. I've been taking it for years, from all sides.

Look, it was a job. That's all it was to me. A job. The money wasn't great, it wasn't even good. But it was OK. And that was OK with me.

It was a job. A job comes along, you take it. I took it.

They approached me. I didn't approach them. They came to me. One at a time. Both of them. I don't know how they found me, but they found me.

I asked them how they found me. It's the kind of thing you like to know. You like to know how people find you. So I asked them. I asked him first because he found me first, or at least I assumed he found me first. I asked him how he found me. He gave me some story or other that made little or no sense to me, so I told him, that story makes little or no sense to me. So he told me another story. It was the same story. It was starting to make sense.

I asked her too. I told her I wanted to know how she found me. So she told me. She told me the same thing he had told me twice, only out of her mouth it sounded different. I didn't know who to believe.

So I believed them both. I believed them both

and I didn't believe either of them. I believed him, but not her. I believed her, but not him. I believed what I wanted to believe.

He approached me first and I didn't ask him what he wanted, he told me. He said nothing, and that said plenty. I guessed what he had on his mind. Call it e.s.p., call it telepathy, call it what you will, I knew. How did I know? He told me. He told me nothing.

She said a little more, and that wasn't much. She said that she had come to see me about the same thing he had seen me about. I told her to go on. So she told me a little more. A little more than nothing. Very little more.

When I pieced together the little that she had told me and everything that he didn't tell me it started to add up to something. I wasn't sure what, though. You're never that sure that early on.

Look, it was a job. And in my position I was in no position to turn down a job. What position was that? I needed a job.

It's rather unorthodox to accept the same job twice, from two different parties, but neither of them seemed to mind. In fact, it was the only way they'd have it. So I accepted the job twice and we were all happy.

Basically it was this. He wanted me to watch her. He also wanted me to watch him and her together. She wanted me to watch him, and she also wanted me to watch her and him together. I was supposed to watch. Just watch. Don't ask any questions, don't bother with conclusions, just watch.

They didn't actually say it in those words, but that's how I read it. I considered the proposition and said, if it's me you want, I'm your man. We shook hands.

So that's how it started. Or at least that's how I thought it started. But it always starts some time before you think it's starting. Way before.

There's no middle here. Just a beginning and an end. There's no middle because it was an open and shut case. I kept my part of the bargain. Did what I was told to do. Kept my eyes on them and didn't ask any questions. Kept my eyes on them and didn't make any judgments, didn't come to any conclusions. That's what I did and that's all I did.

The job was a piece of cake. No complications. I did what I was told to do until they told me to stop.

They thanked me and we settled up. They paid me what we had agreed upon, plus expenses. I took it.

I took it, and I took something else too. I took it because I wanted it. I took it because I needed it. And I took it because I figured I had it coming to me. I took a short nap.

AMERICAN TALES

In a small town a five year old boy has just killed his father. Something just snapped in the child and he felt the need to kill. His father was the only other person in the house at the time. He was in the bathroom, shaving. The boy knew this. He knocked on the bathroom door. ''Open up, Daddy,'' he said. The father opened the door, shaving cream all over his face, Gilette safety razor in hand. The boy shot him with the loaded pistol the father kept in his bedside drawer. The boy shot his father in the head. The bathroom walls are splattered with blood and shaving cream. Mommy will be home soon.

Peggy has a pimple. And a date with Joe. "I can't let Joe see me like this," Peggy thinks. "I'll just die." She doesn't know what to do. After a while she decides to squeeze the pimple. As a result something horrible happens—all her skin comes off her face; she is left with her skeleton exposed. But when Joe comes to call for her he doesn't notice anything. He's so into himself.

At the American Legion bar Crazy Robbie, who lost some of his marbles in Nam, is doing a wild, spastic dance around the pool table and squawking like a chicken. After a few minutes of this, Ernie, the bartender, runs over to Robbie and says, "What the hell do you think you're doing?"

"The fandango," Robbie replies.

Sarah Pickens is a local celebrity. Last week she was on "The Price is Right." She didn't win anything, but there she was—right there on the TV. She even got a kiss from Bob Barker. Now rumor has it that Sarah's thinking of running for Mayor next election. And it looks like she just might win. An awful lot of folks watch "The Price is Right."

Harold is a wife beater. Rita is a battered wife. Rita is not Harold's wife. Harold is not Rita's husband. Harold's wife's name is Mae. Mae is a battered wife. Rita's husband's name is Herb. Herb is a wife beater. Harold and Herb are friends. Rita and Mae are friends.

Ah, friendship!

Miss Emma Hayes is the devil incarnate. She has laced the angel's food cake she has baked for the church's annual bake sale and bazaar with strychnine. Luckily all the townspeople know to avoid Miss Emma's cake, as she is known to be the worst cook in the entire county. So the only person who'll be eating Miss Emma's cake is that traveling salesman just in town for the day. Serves him right.

It turns out that Cal over at the general store is a homosexual, has been all these years. It seems that Cal and his roommate Earl ain't just roommates. That's right—lovers. Yup. And now, what with this news getting out and that new supermarket opening up down the road apiece, Cal is up the creek without a paddle.

"They have some nerve makin' Martin Luther King's birthday a national holiday," says Jack Bemis, founder and president of the Committee to Make Elvis' Birthday a National Holiday.

Dave has been laid off. He was working for a company that manufactured oomph. The oomph industry is in decline, and as a result many oomph-workers are being laid off. What will Dave do? He is forty years old and never learned how to do anything but make oomph.

Why can't they put the oomph back in America? Dave wonders.

MYRON, SAM & GERTRUDE: THREE WAYS TO TELL A STORY

Myron Cohen

This old Jewish fella's walking across the street when all of a sudden a car comes by and runs him over. The fella's lying in the street, unconscious. After a while an ambulance arrives. The ambulance attendants get out, put the fella on a stretcher, and take him inside the ambulance. After a while the fella starts to come to. One of the ambulance attendants asks him, "Mister, are you comfortable?" The fella thinks about it for a minute and says, "Thank God I make a nice living."

Samuel Beckett

To begin, how to begin, to tell the tale of the Old Jew. I will tell the tale of the Old Jew until there is no more to tell. I would rather have remained silent, to await my own end, but they told me, you must go on, you must tell the tale of the Old Jew.

Of the Old Jew there is little to tell. Of how he tried to cross the road, of how he tried to go on, to get to the other side, there is little to tell but the telling.

He was an old acquaintance of mine. From another time, a time before this one, a time long gone. He was older than I and yet I am not young, I was never young. I am old and this tale is older, this tale of the Old Jew who crossed the road.

He had petitioned my assistance, as he was without legs and I had one in proper order. Yet I refused him, told him to go on alone, that I was not of a mind to cross. And he did go on alone, though not without making his contempt known to me. He went on as I watched from my pit by the side of the road.

How can I tell, as I know I must, the rest? Of how he began to crawl across the road, using his bony arms to propel himself millimeter by millimeter. He, braver than I, attempting to cross over to a place no better than the one he had just departed, as I waited, watching. I can't go on.

Yet I must, they say, you must go on with the tale. And so I will, as I must, as I tell of what came next, of the lorry's approach, and how it trampled the unsuspecting Jew.

What came after was the ambulance and its men, the attendants harnessing the Old Jew to a stretcher, taking him inside the ambulance, to await his revival. For days, perhaps weeks, I lose all track of time, I received reports of his condition, one of the attendants bringing the news to my pit every now and again, having been informed of my interest. The end is nearing, I thought, for the Jew, but no, not for the Jew, for my tale. For the Old Jew began to stir, thus prompting one of the attendants to inquire, "Are you comfortable?" And the Jew, dying perhaps but more likely closing, replied, "Thank God I make a nice living."

Gertrude Stein

A Jew is crossing a street. Crossing a street is sweet. A Jew is sweetly crossing. How do you do Mr. Jew. Crossing sweet.

A Jew is a Jew crossing a sweet street. A street is sweet for a Jew to cross but a cross is something else. A street is very sweet but a cross is not Jewish. I do not think.

A Christian is one who crosses himself but a Jew is a Jew when he crosses a street. This is good to know. And so. This is how a Jew crosses.

This one is a Jew who crosses and a car from afar. A Jew who crossed and no longer does. And this one was a crossing Jew.

Accidents are accidental but Jews are on purpose.

A hit and run run over a Jew and go. And so. A Jew is a man with eyes who lies in the street.

An accident and an ambulance and attendants attending. Attending a Jew is something to do.

A man on a stretcher is an accidental Jew and an attendant is one who is saying. Are you comfortable?

Thank you very kindly says the Jew. Thank you kindly I do make a nice living.

MR. CHERCHES
MAILS A LETTER

It's another day. There are so many of them. Seven days in a week, thirty in a month, or thirty-one, or sometimes twenty-eight or twenty-nine, three hundred sixty-five days in a year, and leap years have an extra day, so many days, so much time to fill, twenty-four hours in a day, sixty minutes an hour, sixty seconds a minute, so much time and so little to do.

It's another day and Mr. Cherches can't decide what to do. What to do, what to do, so much time and so little to do, Mr Cherches says to himself. What shall I do today?

Look out the window, Mr. Cherches.

Mr. Cherches looks out the window. It is a bright, sunny day. What shall I do on this bright, sunny day? Mr. Cherches wonders.

One should go out on a bright, sunny day. Bright, sunny days are just right for going out, just as dark, gloomy days are just right for staying in.

Mr. Cherches stayed in yesterday. Yesterday was a dark, gloomy day, and Mr. Cherches stayed in. It was a good day for staying in. But Mr. Cherches hates to do the same thing two days in a row, that makes for a boring existence, and anyway, one should not stay in on a bright, sunny day, for bright sunny days are made for going out.

Go out, Mr. Cherches, go out. It's a bright, sunny day; go out and make the most of it.

But I went out two days ago, Mr. Cherches remembers. And I hate to do the same thing twice in three days, that makes for such a boring existence.

Go out and do something, Mr. Cherches, go out

and do something.

Do something, what a delightful idea, Mr. Cherches thinks. Not just go out, but go out and do something, what a marvelous idea. But what to do, what to do? Mr. Cherches wonders. What shall I do on this bright, sunny day?

Take a walk, take a stroll, see the sights, breathe the air.

But I took a walk last Thursday, I took a stroll on Friday, I saw the sights on Saturday, and I breathed the air on Sunday. I hate to do the same things over and over. It makes for such a boring existence.

Go to the store, look at the pretty women, mail a letter, but do something, Mr. Cherches, do something.

I went to the store on July Fifteenth, I looked at the pretty women on September Twenty-sixth, but I can't remember the last time I mailed a letter, Mr. Cherches remembers. Mailing a letter, that's how I'll spend my day. There's so much time and so little to do that new and unusual experiences make for an exciting existence. I'm going to mail a letter on this bright, sunny day. Hooray!

Mr. Cherches puts on his jacket, Mr. Cherches puts on his cap, Mr. Cherches leaves his apartment and greets the day. It is a bright, sunny day. Mr. Sun smiles at Mr. Cherches. Mr. Cherches smiles at Mr. Sun.

It is such a nice day that Mr. Cherches begins to sing:

I'm going to mail a letter,
I'm going to mail a letter,
Things could be no better,
I'm a real go-getter,
It's a bright, sunny day,
And I hope it stays that way,
'Cause I'm going to mail a letter today, hey-hey,
I'm going to mail a letter today.

Mr. Cherches walks down the block until he reaches the mailbox. Mr. Cherches is going to mail a letter. Mr. Cherches is going to drop a letter in the mailbox. This is the climax of his day.

But wait—there's a problem—Mr. Cherches has neglected one very important item—he doesn't have a letter to mail.

Mr. Cherches, Mr. Cherches, one cannot mail a letter unless one has a letter to mail.

Can it be true? Mr. Cherches wonders. Does one really need to have a letter to mail before one can mail a letter? It sounds logical. But what will I do now?

Write a letter, Mr. Cherches, write a letter.

I guess that's what I'll have to do, Mr. Cherches guesses, I guess I'll have to write a letter. So he rushes home to write a letter, to write a letter to mail.

Who should I write a letter to? Mr. Cherches wonders. I can't write a letter to my friends, that would be silly, I don't have any friends. I can't write a fan letter, there's nobody I want to write a fan letter to. I can't write a letter of complaint, it's a bright, sunny day and one should never write a letter of complaint on a bright, sunny day, one should always save letters of complaint for dark, gloomy days. I guess I'll just have to write a letter to myself.

So Mr. Cherches writes a letter to himself.

> Dear Mr. Cherches,
> I am writing you this letter because I need to write a letter so I can have a letter to mail. I decided to mail a letter today, but when I got to the mailbox I discovered that I did not have a letter to mail. This was bad news, because in order to mail a letter you have to have a letter to mail. So I rushed home in order to write this letter to you so I would have a letter to mail. But you already know all of this because you are me.
> Respectfully,
> Mr. Cherches

Mr. Cherches signs the letter. He folds it and places it in an envelope. He seals the envelope. He writes his own address on it. He puts a stamp on it. The letter is all ready to be mailed. Oh boy!

But wait, Mr. Cherches, take a look out the window.

Mr. Cherches looks out the window. Oh no—it's raining!

That's right, Mr. Cherches, the weatherman is playing a trick on you. It's raining outside, and one should never go out in the rain to mail a letter. You're just going to have to call the whole thing off.

Mr. Cherches begins to cry. It is raining outside, and now I won't be able to mail my letter, he thinks.

My whole day is ruined.

Don't take it so hard, Mr. Cherches, look on the bright side of things. You've already had quite a busy day. You went out to mail a letter, a noble effort in itself, and when you found that you did not have a letter to mail, did you accept defeat? Of course not, you went home and wrote a letter. And quite a good letter at that. And now you have a letter all ready to mail tomorrow. So things have actually worked out quite nicely.

It's true, Mr. Cherches tells himself. I have had quite an exciting day. And not only has today been taken care of, but I also have my tomorrow all cut out for me. There's so much time and so little to do; it's oh so comforting to know that there's something new and exciting for me to do tomorrow.

And Mr. Cherches begins to sing:

> I'll mail my letter tomorrow,
> I'll mail my letter tomorrow,
> I've got no cause for sorrow,
> I've got no cause for sorrow,
> There's so much time,
> And so little to do,
> But I've got something to do tomorrow,
> Something to do tomorrow…

READING COMPREHENSION

I.   Twentieth-century Americans are happier than our ancestors because we have more to be happy about. Also, there are more of us to be happy, so the country is happier as a whole. We have many things to be happy about, but the happiest thing of all is that we are Americans.

Today's American is happier than yesterday's American because life is easier. Our forefathers, those great men who built our nation, did not always have it so easy. Building a nation is hard work, and it doesn't pay very well, so many of our forefathers had to go hungry. Today no American need be hungry. All Americans can eat well because of the sacrifices made by the architects of our great nation. Our great nation was built by many hungry men. George Washington was just one of them.

Life today is also easier than in the past because of the many wonderful inventions that make life easier for all of us. These inventions are the result of American ingenuity. All great inventions are American. Those great American inventors, such as Edison, Bell, and Marconi, were able to make their important discoveries because of the sacrifices of our forefathers. We can watch television and use our electric can openers because Thomas Jefferson often went to bed without supper.

America is the land of opportunity. In America, anybody can be an inventor. For instance, the peanut was invented by a Negro.

Things are very different in Russia. The people in Russia are not happy. In fact, the people in Russia used to be much happier. This is because they used to be ruled by a happy ruler known as the Czar. Now they are ruled by a group of unhappy rulers known as the Communists. Many Russians go to bed without supper. This is very sad, but very true.

1. A good title for this passage would be:

a) Thomas Edison, Inventor
b) Thomas Jefferson, Martyr
c) The Negro Problem
d) Hunger and Happiness

2. The main idea of this passage is:

a) America is good
b) Inventions are good
c) Russia is bad
d) All of the above

3. Thomas Jefferson went to bed without supper because:

a) He went to bed with his slaves
b) He was on a diet
c) He wanted us to be happy
d) Alexander Graham Bell invented the telephone
e) a & c

4. We can watch television because:

a) America is a free country
b) The Russians haven't figured out how to jam the airwaves
c) It was invented by an American
d) None of the above

5. The rulers of Russia are unhappy because:

a) They're Communists
b) They're not American
c) They know they can't win the cold war
d) All of the above

II.   Juanita and her family have recently come to America. America is better than where Juanita comes from. Juanita does not know this, but she will learn, just as she will learn to speak English poorly. Juanita does not understand why she had to leave her old home, but someday she will learn. The first thing she must learn is not to ask questions.

Juanita lives in Cleveland. Cleveland is a city in Iowa. There are many little girls in Cleveland, Iowa, just as there are many little boys where Juanita comes from. Juanita comes from somewhere else. It is better here than where Juanita comes from.

Juanita goes to school in Cleveland. She is in first grade. She is older than most of her classmates, but that is because she is from somewhere else. Most of Juanita's classmates were born in Cleveland, Iowa. Juanita's classmates laugh at her because she pronounces Iowa incorrectly. Juanita says "Ohio." Juanita's classmates laugh when she says "Ohio" instead of "Iowa." Children can be cruel.

Juanita thinks that where she comes from is better than America, because where she comes from the little girls don't laugh at her. She also likes where she comes from better because where she comes from there are many little boys. There are no little boys in Cleveland, Iowa. Someday Juanita will learn that there is no justice in this world.

America is better than where Juanita comes from. Cleveland, Iowa is a very good place for a little girl who doesn't speak English. Next year Juanita will be one year older. Her chest will be fully developed. There will be no little boys to distract her and she will learn to pronounce Iowa correctly. Then she will be promoted to second grade.

1. A good title for this passage would be:

a) A Passage to India
b) A Lesson for Juanita
c) Cleveland, Land of Opportunity
d) Relocation, Its Pros and Cons

2. The main idea of this passage is:

a) America is the best country in the whole world
b) Puberty is no excuse for ignorance
c) A defective education is better than none at all
d) You can't have your cake and eat it too
e) b & d

3. Cleveland is a city in:

a) Ohio
b) Iowa
c) Somewhere else
d) All of the above

4. Juanita comes from:

a) Cuba
b) El Salvador
c) Nicaragua
d) Somewhere else

5. Juanita is in first grade because:

a) She does not speak English
b) There is no justice in this world
c) Her breasts are too small
d) She asks too many questions
e) b & c

III.   Fast food is good for you. Not only is fast food delicious, it is also nutritional. Fast food contains many of the nutrients all human beings require to lead active, healthy lives. Some fast food also contains vitamins, and everybody knows how important vitamins are.

Fast food comes in many forms. The most common kinds of fast food are hamburgers and hot dogs, but there are many other varieties. Fish and Chips has been popular in England for centuries, and now Americans too are enjoying this wonderful, nutritional delicacy. If we take a little time to examine the history of fast food we can learn a lot about many different cultures. For instance, did you know that a Chinaman invented pizza?

There are many people who feel that fast food is not good for you. They have the right to their opinions, because America is a free country, but they are wrong. They are wrong because fast food is good for you.

1. A good title for this passage would be:

a) America, Land of the Free
b) Foods of the World
c) The Truth About Pizza
d) Eating Sensibly

2. The main idea of this passage is:

a) Fast food is good for you
b) Vitamins are important
c) Free speech is an important right which many
   people abuse
d) You *can* have your cake and eat it too

3. Fast food contains:

a) Nutrients
b) Vitamins
c) Fish & Chips
d) Many different cultures

4. America is a free country because:

a) Ignorant people have the right to their opinions
b) Fast food is good for you
c) Fast food is free
d) Americans can eat other people's food
e) a, b & d

IV.   Football is a very popular sport in the United States. Football is also very popular in England, but in England football is a different game. The English are wrong to call their game football, because the game that the English call football is actually the game that we know of as soccer. Soccer uses a round ball, as opposed to football which uses a football. The English also have a game called rugby which uses a ball that looks very much like a football, but rugby is not called football. However, despite the popularity of football in the United States, baseball is still America's favorite pastime.

1. A good title for this passage would be:

a) America's Favorite Pastime
b) A Very Popular Sport
c) England, Land of Mistakes
d) Let's Play Rugby

2. The main idea of this passage is:

a) Football is better than baseball
b) Baseball is better than football
c) America is better than England
d) Baseball is better than Rugby and Soccer put together

3. Rugby and Soccer are:

a) The same
b) Different
c) Both silly games
d) All of the above

4. The English are wrong because:

a) They're not right
b) They're not American
c) They're stupid
d) They use the English language incorrectly

PROBLEMS

1. Johnny wants to buy a bicycle, which costs $200. He has only $120 in his savings account, but he knows of a way to earn the rest of the money he'll need for the bicycle: In his neighborhood there is a man who will pay $15 apiece to have certain individuals bumped off. Johnny goes to see the man, and that day he is given $45 and 3 names. He successfully pulls off all 3 murders, but somehow slips up and leaves a clue. The police catch him and he spends 3 years in a juvenile detention home. When he gets out he still has the money in his savings account and the $45 hit money, but due to inflation the cost of the bicycle has gone up.

If the annual rate of inflation is 8%, and Johnny has been earning 5¾% interest on his savings account, compounded quarterly, how many more people will he have to kill before he can buy the bicycle?

2.   Mr. Smith wants to get from Plainville to Anytown. He can take either the train, the bus, or a plane. The plane is the quickest way. The plane will take Mr. Smith from Plainville to Anytown in 2 hours. But the plane is the most expensive of the 3 choices. The plane costs $200. The cheapest way to get from Plainville to Anytown is by bus. The bus costs only $35. But the bus is also the slowest and least comfortable of the 3 choices. The bus takes 24 hours to get from Plainville to Anytown. The train, on the other hand, is relatively comfortable yet still moderately priced. The train costs $75 and gets from Plainville to Anytown in 15 hours. Mr. Smith decides to take the train.

Mr. Smith kisses his wife in Plainville goodbye. Mr. Smith is going to Anytown to see his other wife. Mr. Smith is a bigamist. Mr. Smith has 2 wives.

Mr. Smith leaves his house in Plainville at 2:00 P.M. His train leaves at 4:00 P.M. It takes Mr. Smith 45 minutes to get from his house to the train station. When he arrives at the train station Mr. Smith is propositioned by a hooker. Since he has some time to kill, and since he has saved $125 by taking the train instead of the plane, he decides to go with her. They go to the Paradise Motel, which is a 5 minute walk from the station. A room at the Paradise Motel costs $10, a room with a clean sheet costs $12. Mr. Smith gives the desk clerk $10. They get to the room and the hooker explains her schedule of fees. Her basic rate is $50, with an additional charge of $15 for "Greek," and she doesn't get into S & M. Mr. Smith decides to pay the extra money for Greek since neither of his 2 wives allow him that particular outlet. He gives the hooker $65 and they both strip. The hooker rubs some K.Y. on Mr. Smith's cock. A tube of K.Y. costs $1.89. Mr. Smith fucks the hooker up the ass. After he is through he asks the hooker if she'll marry him. The hooker declines, explaining that she doesn't get involved with her clients.

Mr. Smith stays in the room with the hooker until 3:30, when he decides it is time to start heading back to the station. He gets to the station at 3:35 and is informed that his train will be 15 minutes late.

The train is actually 20 minutes late, and when it finally comes Mr. Smith gets on and takes a seat.

On the train Mr. Smith meets Miss Doe. They talk for 22 minutes, then Miss Doe tells Mr. Smith that she has a sleeper, which costs an extra $20, but that two can sleep as cheaply as one, as long as they're discreet. Mr. Smith, never one to pass up a bargain, goes with Miss Doe to her sleeper, an upper berth. They do not sleep.

The train pulls into Anytown the next morning at 7:20 A.M. Mr. Smith takes a cab from the station to his house in Anytown. The cab ride takes 18 minutes and costs $3.65, plus a 75¢ tip. When Mr. Smith enters his house he discovers that his wife is not there. She has left a note on the kitchen table explaining that she has turned gay and gone off to live with a woman in Plainville.

Where does that leave Mr. Smith?

3.   A third world nation, which we will call Nation X, has a population problem. Nation X is very small in area. Nation X is the size of Rhode Island, the smallest state in the United States of America. Nation X has a population of 6,420,000. There is not enough food to go around. There is hardly enough room for the people of Nation X to go around. The people of Nation X are always bumping into each other. The people of Nation X do not believe in birth control. The people of Nation X do believe in sex. The population of Nation X is growing by leaps and bounds. Most of the inhabitants of Nation X are very young. Most of them are very hungry. The average family in Nation X is a family of 16. There is never enough milk to go around. Most of the children of Nation X are starving. The United States of America decides to help. They send over a synthetic food product, to feed the children of Nation X. This food product is a chemically synthesized milk substitute called Pseudo-Moo. The United States of America sends 40 tons of Pseudo-Moo to Nation X. 1 lb. of Pseudo-Moo is enough to make 80 8 oz. glasses of artificial milk. An 8 oz. glass of Pseudo-Moo is enough to nourish a child for one 24 hour period. There are 5,136,000 babies in Nation X. The United States of America wants to help. 15 tons of the Pseudo-Moo contain a deadly poison. This poison, when ingested, kills within minutes.

What will the population of Nation X be tomorrow?

4.   Jack's mother sends him out to buy a quart of milk, the cost of which is 60¢. She gives him a dollar and says, "Be sure to bring back 40¢ change." On his way to the market, Jack meets an old man who tries to sell him magic beans. The beans cost 10¢ each, but in order for them to work their magic, the old man tells Jack, you have to buy 3. Jack gives the man the dollar and receives 3 beans and 70¢ change. He gets to the market and realizes that he does not have enough money to purchase a full quart of milk and still return 40¢ to his mother, so instead he buys a pint, the cost of which is 30¢. On his way home he cooks up a scheme. He returns home, gives his mother the milk and the 40¢ and says, "Here's the quart of milk and your change." Jack's mother thanks him and makes a white sauce, which calls for 2 cups of milk. Later, when it comes time to feed Jack's baby brother, she realizes that there is no milk left. She asks Jack to go out and pick up a pint of milk, which costs 30¢. Jack, fearing that once his mother sees the pint of milk, she'll realize that the last "quart" was also a pint, kills his baby brother. He convinces his mother that it would be pointless to buy milk now that the baby brother is dead, but that he knows where to get magic beans for 10¢ apiece, and that all you need is 3 for them to work their magic. "Perhaps," he suggests, "we can plant these beans and wish for baby brother to come back to life." His mother decides that it might be worth a try, so she gives Jack 30¢ and says, "Go buy 3 beans." Jack pretends to go out, pockets the 30¢, and then returns to his mother and gives her

79

the 3 beans he has already purchased. They plant the beans and wish for the baby brother to come back to life, but nothing happens.

If a pint of milk costs the same as 3 useless beans, what is the value of a human life?

5.   Mr. Green has been working for Mr. Cod for 10 years. Mr. Green is upset that after working for the same outfit for 1 decade he earns only $3.50 an hour. Mr. Green has resented his employer for some time, but he has just now gotten up the courage to ask for a raise. Mr. Cod denies Mr. Green a raise on the grounds that he is retarded. When Mr. Green counters by saying that handicapped people deserve a liveable wage just like everybody else, Mr. Cod accuses him of ingratitude and fires him. Mr. Green, unable to face having to tell the bad news to his wife and 3 children, takes his own life by jumping off a bridge. Mr. Cod now has to find a replacement for Mr. Green, another token handicapped individual. He interviews people with all sorts of handicaps, but they all turn the job down based on 2 factors: 1. The job, which entails nothing more than the individual sitting in the firm's reception room wearing a placard that says: MR. COD HIRES THE HANDICAPPED, is wholly undignified, and 2. The pay is too low. Unable to find a bona fide handicapped person, Mr. Cod instead hires his cousin Phil, who is to all appearances completely normal, though he has been unemployed for 2 years. Mr. Cod offers Phil $3.25 an hour, which Phil gladly accepts since any wage, however small, is preferable to the indignity of unemployment. However, several months later, Phil learns that his predecessor had been paid at a higher rate. When he complains to Mr. Cod of this discrepancy, Mr. Cod

explains that Mr. Green was retarded, and there-
fore was entitled to more money.

*Assuming the validity of Mr. Cod's argument,
what would Phil have to do to earn a raise?*

6.   A man drives a car at 50 miles per hour. The car gets 17.5 miles to the gallon. The man is going from point A to point B. Point B is 326 miles from point A. The car is a convertible. Point B is in another country. The man has just killed his wife. The car is a Buick convertible. The man has blood on his hands. It is 9:00 P.M. The man has stabbed his wife 6 times in the chest. The car's gas tank holds 20 gallons. The wife's corpse is at point A. The man has left point A with a ¾ full tank. Half-way between point A and point B is the Sunflower Diner. A hamburger at the Sunflower Diner costs $1.35. A side order of french fries costs 65¢. A coke costs 45¢. When the man in the Buick convertible reaches the Sunflower Diner he decides he'd like a coffee to go. He enters the diner. He orders a coffee to go. Light and sweet. The coffee costs 35¢. He pays for it and takes it out. He gets into his car again and starts it up. He drives 12 miles, this time at 35 MPH, then decides to take a sip of his coffee. There has been a mistake, the coffee is black no sugar. The man drives back to the Sunflower Diner. He stabs Ethel, the waitress responsible for the coffee mixup. He stabs her 6 times in the chest. He gets back into his car and once again heads toward point B, this time at 55 MPH. He runs out of gas along the way.

Where is he?

7.   A man goes to a fancy restaurant and orders a steak dinner. The waiter asks the man whether he'd like the 12 oz. or the 16 oz. steak. What's the difference? the man asks. The 16 oz. steak is larger, the waiter replies. I know that, the man says, I mean what's the difference in price? The 16 oz. steak is more expensive, the waiter replies. I figured as much, the man says, how much more? The 16 oz. steak costs $2 more than the 12 oz. steak, the waiter replies. All right, the man says, I'll take the 16 oz. steak. Would you like that with a baked potato or sauteed mushrooms? the waiter asks. What's the difference? the man says. Mushroom is a fungus, potato is a tuber, the waiter replies. I know that, the man says, I mean what's the difference in price? The mushrooms costs $1 more than the potato, the waiter replies. All right, I'll take the mushrooms, the man says. Would you like your salad with Italian dressing or bleu cheese? the waiter asks. Do I get a salad? the man asks. If you'd like one, but it's a la carte, the waiter replies. How much does it cost? the man asks. It all depends, the waiter says. On what? the man asks. The dressing, the waiter replies. What's the difference, the man asks. The Italian dressing is basically oil and vinegar with herbs and spices, while the bleu cheese is made with bleu cheese, the waiter replies. In price, the man says. The bleu cheese is more expensive, the waiter replies. How much? the man asks. The bleu cheese costs 50¢ extra, the waiter replies. All right, give me the blue cheese, the man says. Will there be anything else? the waiter asks. No, the man says.

The waiter goes away and some time later he returns with the man's meal. He has gotten the entire order wrong. He brings the man a 12 oz. steak, a baked potato, and a salad with Italian dressing.

What's the difference?

DOODADS

Doodad 1
The Invention of Catch

A man threw a stone at a bird, and the bird threw it back, and the man threw it back at the bird, and the bird threw it back at the man, and the man once again threw the stone at the bird, and the bird once again threw the stone at the man, and the man threw it back, and the bird threw it back, and the man and the bird threw the stone back and forth.

Doodad 2

These are the ones that go in but never come out. The ones that go in, stay for a short time, then come out. The ones that go in, stay for a long time, then come out. The ones that go in, take one look, and come right out.

These are the ones that I think about.

These are the ones that come and go as they please. The ones that come and go as they are told. They are told to come and go as they please. They are told to please come and go.

These are the ones that can please me. These are the ones that can come and go. The ones that can come and go as they please. These are the ones that I think about.

And thinking about them pleases me.

Doodad 3
No Name

She came and she went. She came and she went. She came and she went and she didn't have a name.

She came. She came. She came without a name. She went and she came. She went and she came. She went and she came and she didn't have a name.

She had a face. She had a voice. She had a face she had a voice but she didn't have a name. She went and she came and she didn't have a name.

She came. She came. She came without a name. She came and she came and she came. And she went. She went. She went without a name.

She came. She came. With a voice and a face she came. She came and she came and she didn't have a name.

She didn't have a name. She came. With a voice she came. With a face she came. And she went she went she went without a name.

She went without a name she came. She came without a name. She came and she came and she came. And she went. She went. With a voice and a face and a face and a voice and she went and she came no name no name.

Doodad 4
No Crime

The patterns in the key sent in by the sea made the sun seem an unusual one. He'd been watching for clues, and he tried to moo for them too. The scene was eerie, it was weary of a murder. He had tried to grease the police, but they put him off. They didn't want an outside dick to stick his nose in. So, fearing a kick from the cops, and throwing a bone to his woes, he decided to go it alone. Only, there was a problem — his private erection collection was occupying his attention.

He walked through the sense of the fence, past the dead beside the shed. Inside the victim was found, knife wound in his chest. On a nearby desk lay a floor plan, covered with sand and cream from an abandoned evergreen. On the map, in one corner, was a mourner, surrounded by a broken circle. The mourner held an arrow, which pointed to a narrow window. He looked out, thought he heard a shout, and ran to take a closer look. The tree shook and he thought he glimpsed a familiar shape. An apparent rape in the leaves kept him probing. But no, it was an illusion, the conclusion to a futile search. There was nothing in the tree, there was no crime. The cops, ungreased, ungrimed, had set him up for their own good time. I'll get even with the cops, he swore, and he swallowed the key, and the sun followed, and the earth froze, and the cops died, and the mourner in the corner cried.

Doodad 5

It was the best of times, it was the worst of times. It was the last of times, it was the first of times. It was the fast of times, it was the thirst of times. It was the blast of times, it was the burst of times.

It was the past of times. A time for all good men to come to the aid of their country. A time for all bad men to be good boys. It was a time when there was no such thing as a bad boy.

Now that time is gone. Now bad boys abound. Now a good man is hard to find.

Now everybody is looking for a good time. Now everybody is looking for a better time. Now everybody is looking for the best of times.

Doodad 6
Walking in Circles

We were walking in circles, she and I, we were walking in circles. How long can this go on, I heard a little voice say.

We were walking in circles. I was walking in circles, she was walking in smaller circles. We were walking in concentric circles. How long can this go on, I heard a little voice say.

We were walking in circles, she and I, we were walking in concentric circles. I was walking clockwise, she was walking counter-clockwise. I heard a little voice say, how long can this go on.

She was screaming. She was screaming in circles. I started screaming in larger circles. We were screaming in concentric circles. How long can this go on, I heard a little voice say.

I was screaming clockwise, she was screaming counter-clockwise. I heard a little voice say, how long can this go on.

A little voice was screaming in circles; another little voice was screaming in smaller circles; two little voices were screaming in concentric circles. One was screaming clockwise, the other was screaming counter-clockwise. How long can this go on, I heard a little voice say, how long can this go on.

And the other little voice screamed back, it can go on forever.

Doodad 7

Oh, I'm so ugly, so very ugly, so says the old blind woman as she stares out the window, thinking it's a mirror because she's the old blind woman on the other side.

Doodad 8

He buttons his coat, he unbuttons his coat, he zips his coat, he unzips his coat, he snaps his coat, he unsnaps his coat, he buckles his coat, he unbuckles his coat, he twist ties his coat, he untwist ties his coat, he glues his coat, he unglues his coat, he burns his coat, he unburns his coat, he sautees his coat, he unsautees his coat, he seduces his coat, he unseduces his coat, he fucks his coat, he unfucks his coat, he considers his coat, he unconsiders his coat, he contemplates his coat, he uncontemplates his coat, he postulates his coat, he unpostulates his coat, he hypothesizes his coat, he unhypothesizes his coat, he analyzes his coat, he unanalyzes his coat, he formulates his coat, he unformulates his coat, he publishes his coat, he unpublishes his coat, he criticizes his coat, he uncriticizes his coat, he models his coat, he unmodels his coat, he dons his coat, he undons his coat, he wears his coat, he wears his coat out, it is cold out, too cold for his worn out coat, and he dies, he dies of exposure in his undyed unblue coat.

Doodad 9

If there is a choice between the one and the other, always take the other.

If there is a choice between this one and that one, always take that one.

If there is a choice between that one and the other one, toss a coin.

If you can't find a coin, use a daisy. You know — she loves me, she loves me not. That one, the other one, that one, the other one, that one...

Which one did you end up with? This one? That's impossible. This one wasn't one of the choices. The choice was between that one and the other one. That one, the other one, that one, the other one, that one, the other one... She loves me, she loves me not, she loves me...

What's that? You couldn't find a daisy, so you used a coconut.

Doodad 10

I can see the stars at night, I can see the sun when I wake, I can see you with your hands in my pockets, but I don't feel a thing.

UNFAMILIAR TALES

An Unfamiliar Face

I was staring at an unfamiliar face. I did not know this face. To me this face was unfamiliar. Unfamiliar and intriguing.

"Do I know you?" I asked her.

"Of course, darling," she said. "Of course you know me."

"But not your face," I said.

"But not my face," she affirmed.

An Unfamiliar Race

I was running in an unfamiliar race. Everything about this race was unfamiliar. Except my opponent. I knew my opponent. My opponent was familiar.

She had taken an early lead, but I finally caught up with her.

"This race is unfamiliar," I told her, through huffs and puffs.

"I thought you'd never notice," she said, and once again drew ahead of me.

Another Unfamiliar Race

On our last expedition we encountered an unfamiliar race. "This is startling," I said to my companion. "I thought for sure that all the races of the world had been discovered by now, yet this one is completely unfamiliar."

"Well," she replied, "this race is obviously a well kept secret."

An Unfamiliar Lace

I found a shoelace on the floor. It was not one of mine. As far as I could tell, it was not one of hers. It was a man's lace. The kind of shoelace you'd find on a man's shoe. I picked it up. I showed it to her. I dangled it in front of her face and said, "Whose lace is this?"

"I don't know," she said, "but I hope he gets home all right."

An Unfamiliar Case

The chief assigned me to an unfamiliar case. I was unfamiliar with the particulars of this case. When I asked her for some specifics, explaining that I couldn't solve the case unless I had some leads, she replied, "First find the case, *then* solve it."

An Unfamiliar Grace

The woman looked familiar. So I followed her. I followed her for blocks and blocks. I kept looking at her, but I still couldn't be sure.

"Excuse me, Miss," I said, "but could you tell me your name?"

She turned to me and in an unfamiliar voice said, "Grace."

An Unfamiliar Pace

There was something different about her heartbeat. Her heart was beating at an unfamiliar pace.

What could be the cause of this unfamiliar pace? I wondered. Could it be something I said? Something I did?

I was reluctant to broach the subject, so I ruminated for a while on the beating of her heart. After some time had passed I finally decided to ask her the cause of the change, but by that time it was no longer necessary, as her heart had already returned to a more familiar beat.

An Unfamiliar Taste

I was quite familiar with her cooking, so you can imagine my surprise when I happened upon an unfamiliar taste.

"Something tastes unfamiliar," I said to her.

"I tried something different this time," she said, "Do you like it?"

"I guess so," I said. "But what's different?"

"I'm not sure," she said. "But if you like it I'll make it again."

An Unfamiliar Gaze

I saw her staring out the window, with an unfamiliar gaze. It was a gaze that I had never seen before. I wondered what could be responsible for her unfamiliar gaze.

"What are you staring at?" I asked her.

"It's the most amazing thing," she replied. "Come, take a look for yourself."

I joined her at the window and took a look. She was right. It was truly the most amazing thing I had ever seen.

An Unfamiliar Phase

I was going through an unfamiliar phase.
"I don't know you any more," she told me.
"You've become a stranger."
"Don't worry," I said. "It's just a phase."

An Unfamiliar Phrase

We were having a conversation, when all of a sudden I uttered an unfamiliar phrase. I became flustered, began to apologize. "I don't know where that phrase come from," I told her. "I assure you, it's an unfamiliar phrase."

"It's nothing to be ashamed of," she told me. "According to Chomsky, it's perfectly normal to utter an unfamiliar phrase every once in a while."

An Unfamiliar Maize

The last time I dined at the reservation Pocahontas served an unfamiliar maize. "This maize is unfamiliar," I told her. "I do not know this maize."

"Oh, cut the corn," she replied.

An Unfamiliar Vase

The flowers were sitting in an unfamiliar vase. I did not know that vase. To me that vase was unfamiliar. So I questioned her. I questioned her about the vase.

"Where did you get that vase?" I asked her.

"What vase?" she asked.

"*That* vase," I said, pointing at the vase in question.

"Oh, *that* vase," she said. "I thought you gave it to me."

An Unfamiliar Ace

All right. This time I had her beaten. I was holding four kings and the ace of spades.

So I wagered everything.

And lost.

"Four aces," she said.

She showed me her hand. Four aces. Ace of clubs, ace of hearts, ace of diamonds, and a fourth ace. An unfamiliar ace.

An Unfamiliar Place

So there we were, the two of us, once again, in an unfamiliar place.

EATING SOUP

We're great fans of Campbell's soup. We try all the different varieties. They occasionally come up with a new variety, and when we see a new variety of Campbell's soup at the supermarket, we invariably try it. We trust Campbell's soup. We trust the Campbell's people to make a good product. Rarely do they disappoint us. We love condensed soup.

We do, however, each have our personal favorites. Mine are: Bean with Bacon, Turkey Vegetable, and Clam Chowder. Hers are Chicken Noodle, Vegetarian Vegetable, and Cream of Celery. Sometimes we mix and match, as the Campbell's people suggest in the helpful hints section on the back of the label. We have tried many combinations, among them Chicken Clam Noodle Chowder and Vegetarian Beef Noodle Vegetable. Obviously the names of the original soups become unimportant—when we mix Vegetarian Vegetable and Beef Noodle we create a paradoxical soup. Paradoxical but delicious. Umm, umm good.

Tonight we are going our separate ways—I am eating an old favorite, Bean with Bacon, one of the Manhandlers, and she is having Stockpot.

She has this annoying habit of reading at the table. She reads Reader's Digest Condensed Books. She is reading an abridged version of *Anna Karenina*. The folks at Reader's Digest have pared down Tolstoi's masterpiece to forty-seven pages. They have no doubt selected the meatiest yet most tasteful sections.

I figure as long as she's going to read while we eat, I can watch TV. I usually watch *Green Acres* while I eat. Tonight's episode has something to do with Mrs. Douglas' hotcakes recipe and Arnold the Pig, but I'm not sure what the connection is.

"How do you expect me to read with the TV on," she says.

"C'est la vie," I say, hoping she'll put down the book.

"You're a prick," she says, hoping I'll turn off the TV.

The *TV Guide* describes tonight's episode with flawless concision: "A mixup involving Mrs. Douglas' hotcakes recipe and Arnold the Pig tries Oliver's patience." The *TV Guide* is able to condense thirty minutes of television into one sentence. The medium is the message. The *TV Guide* is America's largest selling periodical.

Anyway, we're at a standstill. She continues reading, I keep watching TV.

"Green Acres is the place for me," I tell her.

"St. Petersburg is where I'd rather stay," she replies.